LITTLE MISS SPARKLE

originated by Roger Hargreaves

Written and illustrated by Adam Hargreaves

PSS!
PRICE STERN SLOAN
An Imprint of Penguin Random House

Little Miss Sparkle was full of life.

She was so full of the joys of life that she glowed and glittered and sparkled just like the night sky.

She loved to chat and play.

She loved singing and games.

But the thing she liked most was dancing.

She danced with everyone, and she danced with anyone.

She danced with Mr. Greedy.

She danced with Mr. Skinny.

She danced with Mr. Clumsy, even though he stepped on her toes!

The more she danced, the happier she became.

And the happier she became, the more she glowed.

And the more she glowed, the more she sparkled.

Which was rather handy on the way home late at night.

Everything was just splendid . . .

That is, until last week.

On Monday, it rained and Little Miss Sparkle
found that Little Miss Naughty had cut holes in her
umbrella, and she got wet.

On Tuesday, Little Miss Bossy told her to stop singing.

"Your singing is giving me a headache!" barked Little Miss Bossy.

On Wednesday, Mr. Uppity drove through a puddle and soaked her from head to toe.

On Thursday, Mr. Sneeze gave her his cold.

And on Friday, Mr. Rude told her she looked ridiculous when she danced.

What a miserable week!

By the weekend, Little Miss Sparkle was feeling just as miserable.

She did not feel like chatting or singing or playing games.

She did not even feel like dancing.

And there was something else about her that had changed.

She no longer glowed.

She no longer glittered.

She had lost her sparkle!

"I've lost my sparkle!" she cried in dismay, when Mr. Silly turned up at her house.

"Oh dear," said Mr. Silly. "Where did you last see it?"

"Maybe it's under the stairs?" he suggested.

But when he looked, there was no sparkle.

Well, there wouldn't be, would there?

That would be silly.

"That's just silly," said Little Miss Sparkle with a smile.

Mr. Silly thought long and hard.

How could he help Little Miss Sparkle?

And then he had an idea.

He ran out to the store and bought some glitter.

"That's not quite the same thing," said Little Miss Sparkle with a giggle.

"Maybe your sparkle is not lost, maybe it's playing hide-and-seek!" exclaimed Mr. Silly.

Mr. Silly rushed around the house looking in all the cupboards and under the bed and even in the fridge.

But, of course, he did not find the sparkle.

"You are silly!" laughed Little Miss Sparkle.

And she laughed and she laughed and she laughed.

And the more she laughed, the more she glowed.

And the more she glowed, the more she sparkled.

She was soon sparkling from head to toe.

And beaming from cheek to cheek.

"That's better!" cried Mr. Silly. "You're back to your old self."

"Look! Even my toes are sparkling," said Little Miss Sparkle.

"Twinkle toes!" cried Mr. Silly.

Little Miss Sparkle was so happy to have her sparkle back, she danced around the kitchen.

And then she danced around the kitchen table.

She even danced *on* the table!

On his way home, Mr. Silly decided he needed some sparkle of his own.

He stopped at the store, but did not go in.

He was afraid of seeming foolish because he did not know whether to ask for a can of sparkle or a box of sparkle.

Silly old Mr. Silly.

Everyone knows sparkle comes in a tube!